MUSHROOM CITY

Hunter 3 was on course
from Earth to Planet Marco.

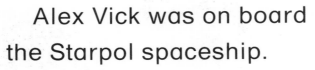

Alex Vick was on board
the Starpol spaceship.
"My job is to make friends with
the people of Marco," said Vick.
"The problem is,
they don't trust Earth people."

Sun Lee was a Starpol
Weapons Officer.
Her job was to guard Vick on
his visit to Marco.

"There's Planet Marco," said Anna.
Captain Peck gave the order,
"Get ready to land."
"We may be in danger when
we get there," said Lee.
"We must all watch out!"

Hunter 3 landed near a big city.

"These people look very odd," said Anna.

"We must look very odd to them," said Lee. "Maybe that is why they don't trust us."

"Here comes Torno," said Vick.
"He is the chief Marcon."

Alex Vick talked to Torno.

"He seems friendly," said Peck.

"They all **seem** friendly," said Lee,

"but they may change suddenly."

The Starpol crew were taken
into the city.

"Look at those houses,"
said Mary.

"They are like mushrooms!"

They came to a big hall in
the middle of the city.

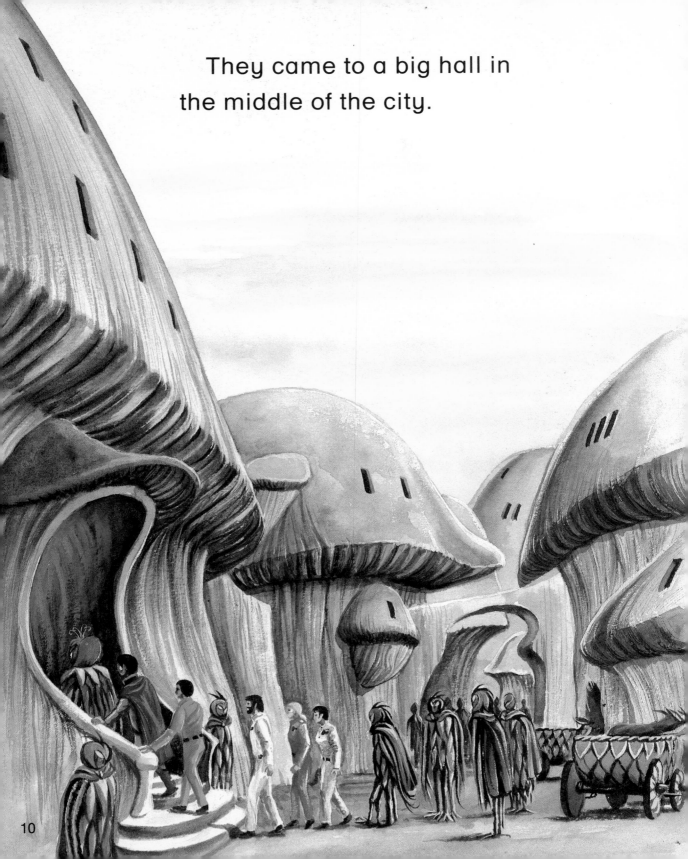

Torno led them into the hall.
"The Marcons are going to give us
a grand feast," said Vick.

11

They all sat down to eat.

"Is this meat?" asked Mary.

"Yes, it is," said Anna.

"Marcons won't eat plants."

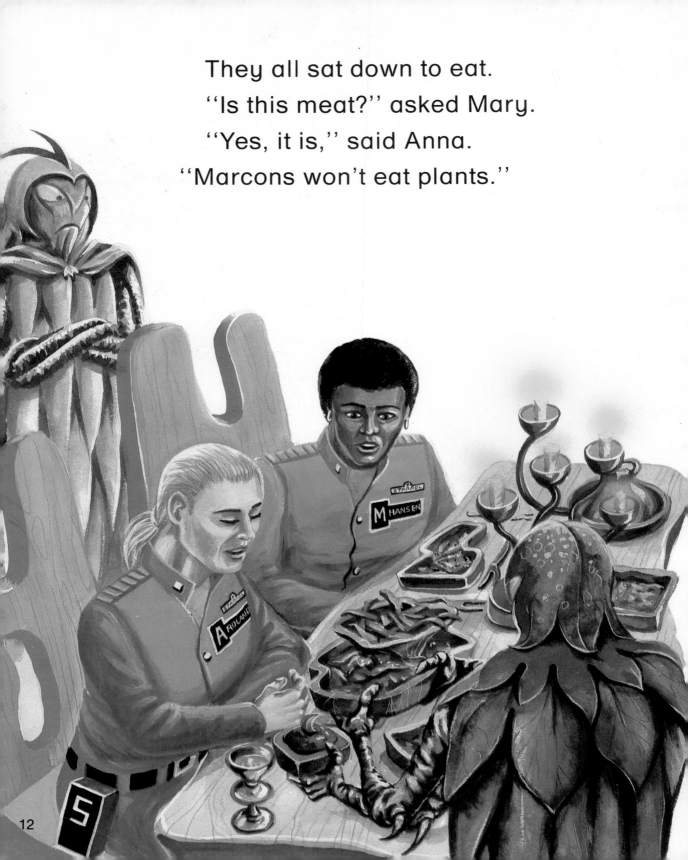

Alex Vick sat beside Torno
and talked to him.

Captain Peck and Sun Lee
sat the other side of Torno.
Two guards stood behind them.

After dinner, Vick got up.
"Marcons," he said. "I bring you
a message from the people on Earth.
We want to be friends with you."

"The guards are watching us,"
whispered Peck.

"I don't like it," said Lee.
She told Peck what she planned to
do if there was trouble.

Suddenly, the big plant
behind Alex Vick snapped shut.
He was trapped inside!

"Look out!" yelled Lee.
Peck and Lee dived to the floor.
The guards' arms lashed out over
their heads like whips.

Mary and Anna were not ready.
The guards closed their arms
around them, holding them tight.

Lee fired her laser gun at
the tree of lights.

The tree crashed into
the middle of the hall and
the lights went out.
Lee ran for the door.

She dived down the steps
outside the hall.

The guards' arms missed her and
wrapped round each other!

Then Lee fired her laser gun at
the trunk of the mushroom hall.
Smoke came from the trunk.

The walls of the hall
begin to fall.
The roof was coming down.
The Marcons were very frightened.

Captain Peck cut the plant open
so that Vick could escape.

"Get out the back way, quickly!"
said Peck.

Vick ran out from the back
of the hall.
A guard was waiting there!
Lee came up behind the guard
and knocked him out.

25

Inside the hall the Marcons
were running away.
Peck helped Anna and Mary.
"We must get out of here!"
he yelled.

"Help!" shouted Anna.

"I can't move!"

She was trapped under the roof.

Mary grabbed Anna's hands and pulled her out.

Peck, Anna and Mary ran down
the steps from the hall.

But Torno and the Marcon guards
were all around them.

There was no way to escape!

Suddenly, a carriage rushed out
from behind the hall.
Vick was sitting in it and
Lee was driving.
''Quick, jump in!'' she yelled.

"Hold on tight!" called Lee.
She drove the carriage as fast
as she could.

Torno and his guards dived
out of the way.

Lee drove the carriage
out of the city at full speed.
  "Everyone into the ship!"
yelled Peck.
  "Get ready for take off!"

Hunter 3 took off fast.

Alex Vick looked down at Planet Marco.

"I'll come back one day," he said. "I'll make friends with the Marcons somehow!"